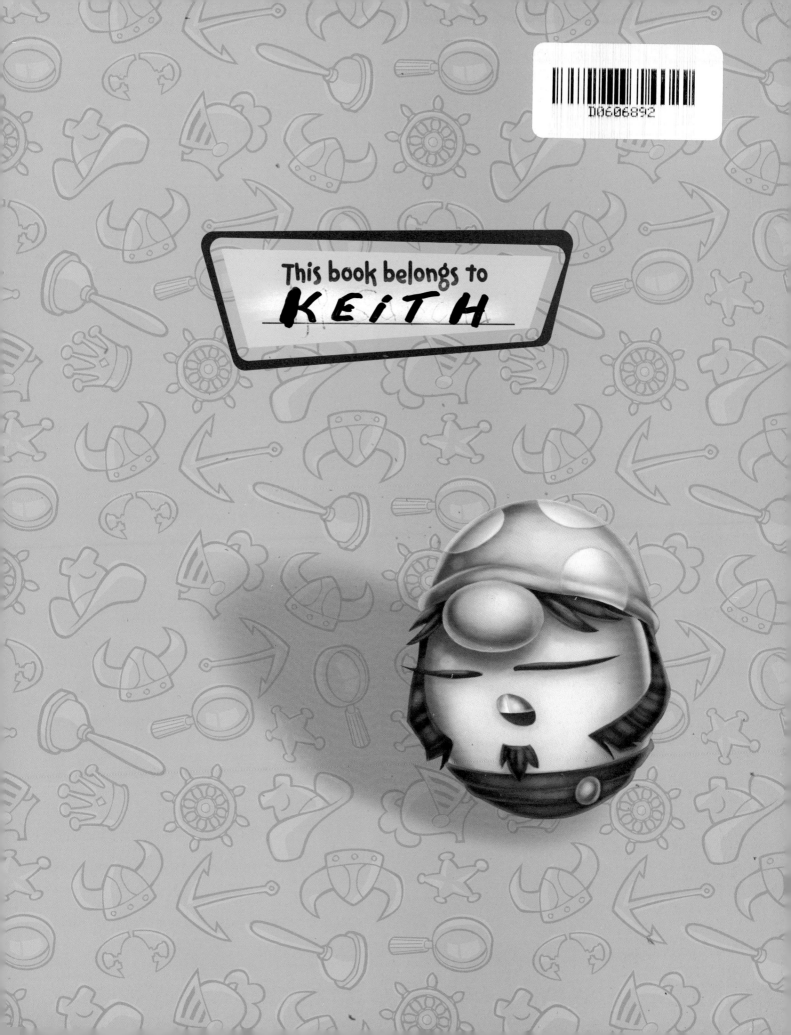

This book belongs to
**KEITH**

# THREE PIRATES AND A DUCK

## A Lesson in Sharing

by
Doug Peterson

Illustrated by
Robert Vann
and Casey Jones

SCHOLASTIC INC.

New York  Toronto  London  Auckland  Sydney
Mexico City  New Delhi  Hong Kong  Buenos Aires

# Ahoy there, matey!

Let me tickle your ears with a strange, delicious
tale about the Pirates Who Don't Do Anything.

If you can believe it, these pirates hardly ever sailed anywhere. That's why
they've never been to Greenland. They've never buried treasure in St. Louie
or St. Paul. And they've never even been to Boston in the fall.

*Arrrgh!* The Pirates Who Don't Do Anything usually lie around all day
watching reruns on TV and eating twisted cheese curls—but not today!

"Is our ship moving?" asked Pa Grape, the pirate captain.

"Hey, I think it is," said Mr. Lunt. "Didn't you tie our ship to the dock last night?" he asked Larry the Cucumber.

"Did I do *what?*" asked Larry.

"Did you tie our ship to the dock?" repeated Mr. Lunt.

"Oops," said Larry. "I thought you asked me to tie the ship to the *duck*."

"Quack!"

(That's duck talk for "this rope is itchy.")

Shiver me timbers! During the night, their ship had drifted out to sea. There was nothing but water all around—except for one thing far, far away. As the ship floated closer to this thing, Larry put a telescope up to his eye.

"I don't see anything," Larry said.

"That's because you're wearing a pirate patch on *both* eyes," said Mr. Lunt.

"Oh—right—good point," Larry admitted. Then he flipped up one of the patches and stared at the thing in the water.

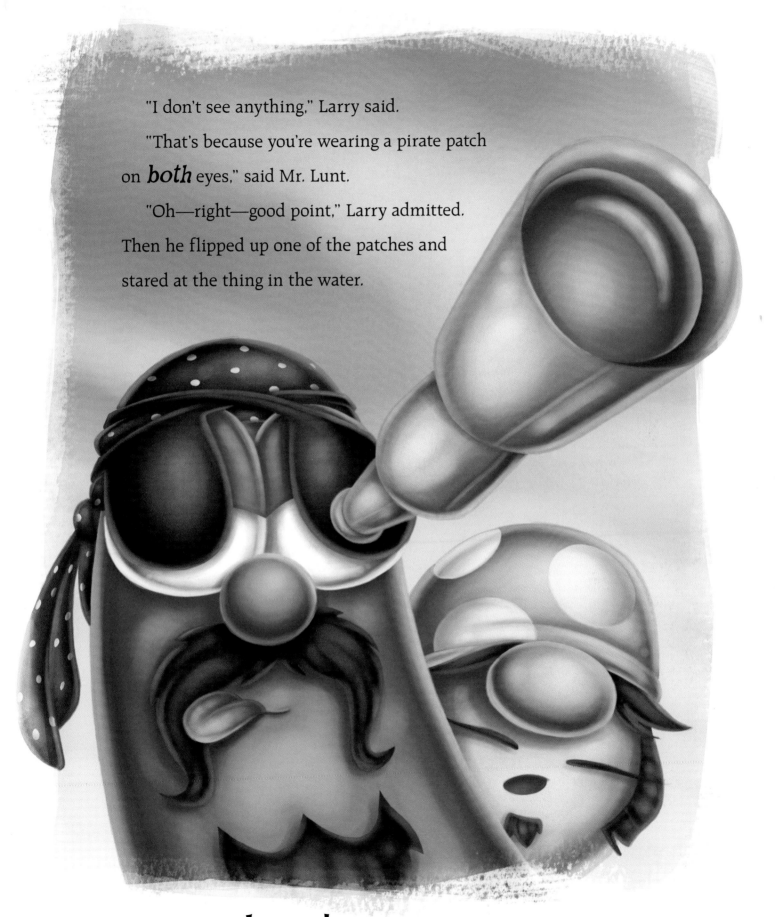

This thing was **huge!** But it wasn't a whale. It wasn't a giant squid. It wasn't even King Kong in a bathing suit. It was . . .

# . . . a giant cookie!

"Thar she blows!" Larry shouted.

"Well I'll be," said Pa Grape. "It's Moby Chip,

the largest chocolate chip cookie on the Seven Seas!"

"It's making me hungry," said Mr. Lunt.

So the pirates harpooned the monster cookie and hauled it on board the ship. But that is when the trouble started.

"I saw the cookie first, so it's **mine**," said Larry.

"But *I'm* the one who knew it was called Moby Chip," said Pa Grape, "so it's **mine**."

"But *I* have the sweetest tooth on the chip . . . er . . . I mean ship," added Mr. Lunt, "so it's **mine!**"

As you can see, matey, God had given them a good thing—a giant chocolate chip cookie. But these pirates did not want to share it. They began to fight over the cookie in the wackiest way—with dirty laundry!

Pa Grape filled his cannon with unwashed pirate clothes. "Take this, you dirty rats!" he declared.

# KABOOM!

"Oh yeah?" shouted
Mr. Lunt. "Take this!"
# KAPOW!

"That's nothing!" yelled Larry. "I'll get you!"
Larry closed his eyes and waited for his
cannon to fire the dirty clothes, but the duck
turned it around on him.
# KABLOOEY!

*"Arrrgh!"* Larry scowled.
(That is pirate talk for "never
trust a duck.")

The fighting went on and on. Socks, shirts, and eye patches were flying everywhere.

Finally, Pa Grape shouted, "I am king of the cookie!" as he planted a flag in the center of the giant cookie.

"Hey, wait, Cap'n," said Mr. Lunt. "Am I seeing things, or is our ship filling with water?"

Mr. Lunt was right. The giant cookie was so heavy
that it was sinking their ship! **Arrrgh!**
"What do we do? What do we do?" Larry
shouted, running around in circles until he crashed
into the mainmast.

"There's only one thing we can do," said Pa Grape. The others turned and looked him in the eye—even the duck! "We must *share* the cookie." So the Pirates Who Don't Do Anything actually *did* something. They shared a good thing from God. Together, they began to gobble up the chocolate chip cookie, trying to make it smaller and lighter.

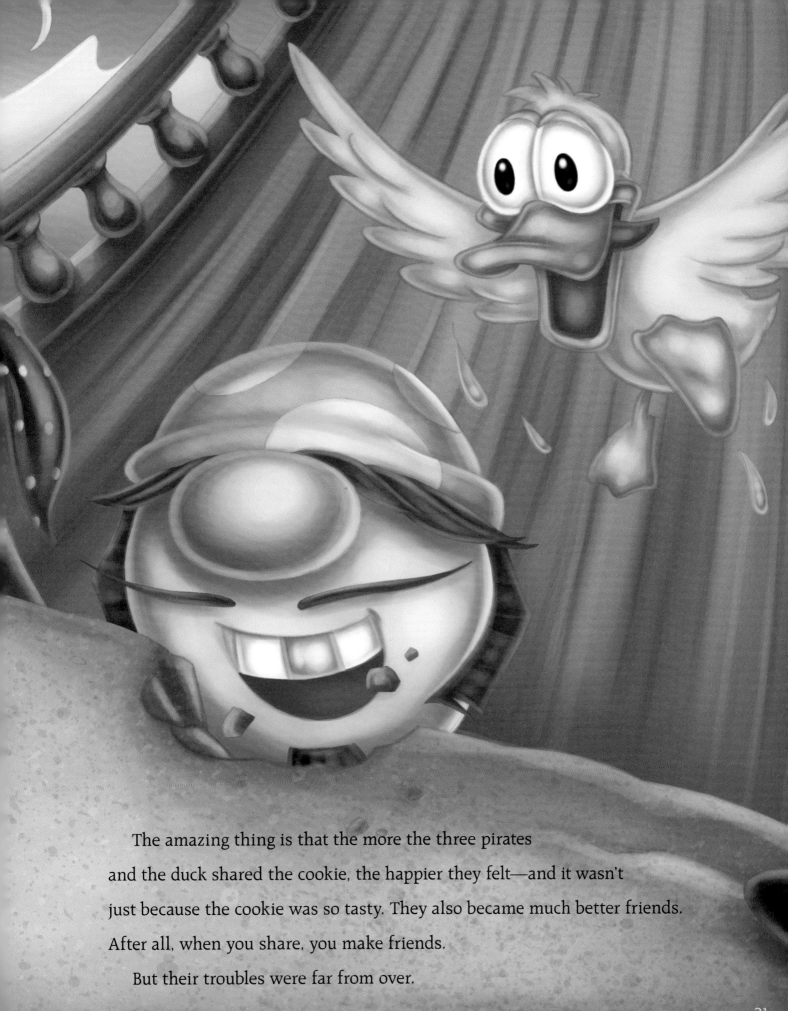

The amazing thing is that the more the three pirates
and the duck shared the cookie, the happier they felt—and it wasn't
just because the cookie was so tasty. They also became much better friends.
After all, when you share, you make friends.

But their troubles were far from over.

"*Arrrgh!*" growled Pa Grape. "We can't eat the cookie fast enough. The ship is still sinking!"

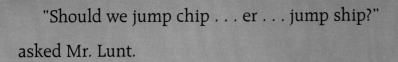

"Should we jump chip . . . er . . . jump ship?"
asked Mr. Lunt.

"I thought the captain was supposed to go down
with the chip," Larry added, looking at Pa Grape.

While the pirates tried to figure out what to
do, another ship suddenly sailed alongside them.

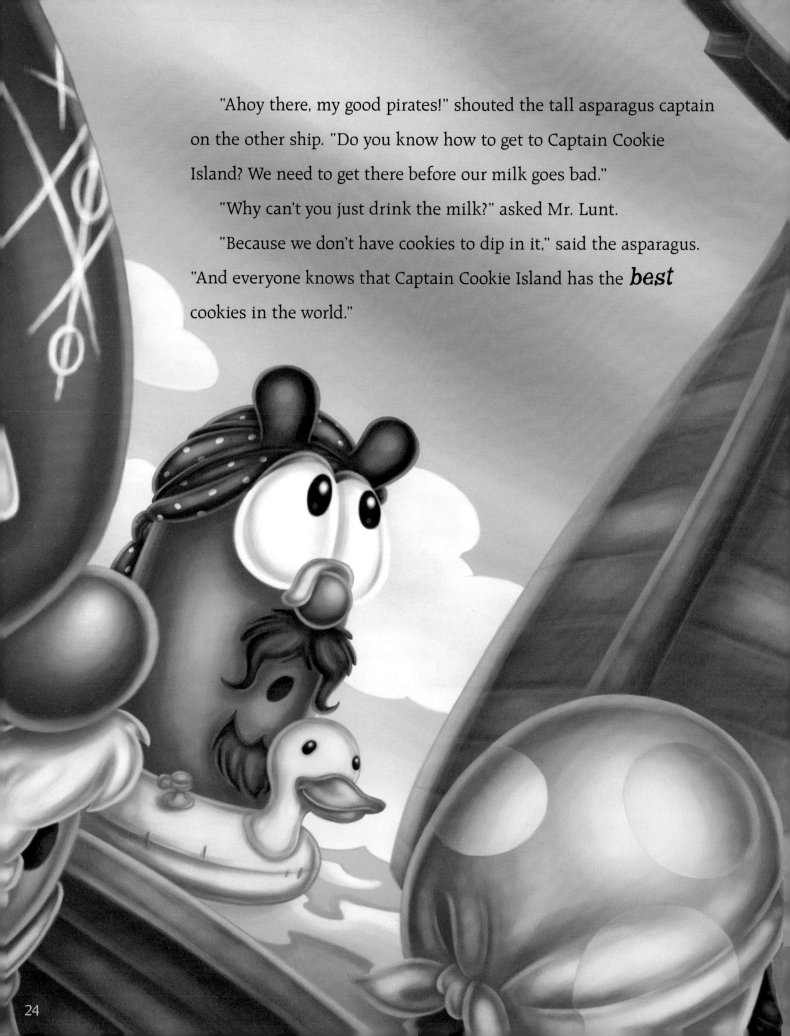

"Ahoy there, my good pirates!" shouted the tall asparagus captain on the other ship. "Do you know how to get to Captain Cookie Island? We need to get there before our milk goes bad."

"Why can't you just drink the milk?" asked Mr. Lunt.

"Because we don't have cookies to dip in it," said the asparagus. "And everyone knows that Captain Cookie Island has the *best* cookies in the world."

Mr. Lunt looked at Pa Grape who

looked at Larry who looked at the duck who just quacked.

"This is your day!" declared Pa Grape. "We have the *biggest* cookie

in the world—Moby Chip! We'll share it with you!"

The asparagus's eyes grew wide when he spotted the huge cookie. "If you're going

to share your cookie, then we'll share our milk," he said. "Prepare to be boarded!"

So the asparagus and his sailors swarmed onto the pirates' ship. As everyone shared, the cookie got smaller and the ship was saved. The pirates were also happy because they had made new friends.

"Yo-ho-ho and a carton of milk!" Larry shouted. He dipped a piece of cookie in milk and handed it to the duck.

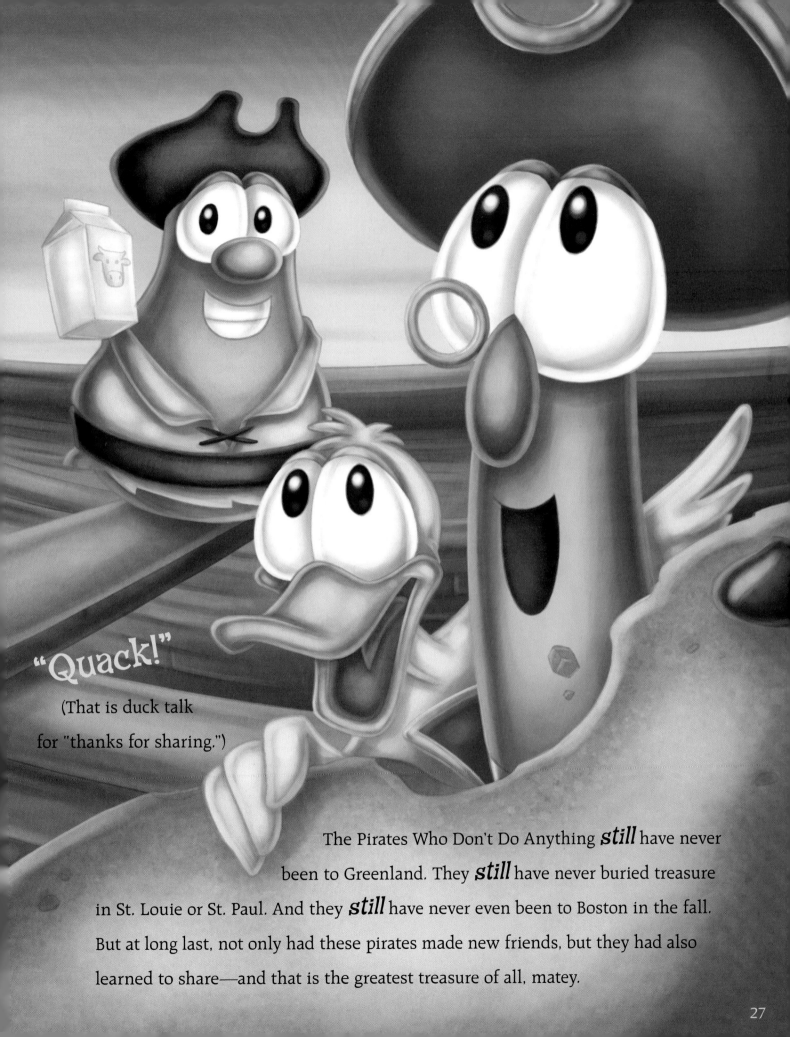

"Quack!"

(That is duck talk
for "thanks for sharing.")

The Pirates Who Don't Do Anything *still* have never
been to Greenland. They *still* have never buried treasure
in St. Louie or St. Paul. And they *still* have never even been to Boston in the fall.
But at long last, not only had these pirates made new friends, but they had also
learned to share—and that is the greatest treasure of all, matey.

So come with us. The Lord will give us good things.
We'll share them with you.

Numbers 10:32